S.N.O.T (Selheeva Norkhov (

BOOK 1. THE LEAKIN(

How to read these words if you a1

Sell as in sell, *hee* as in he-he, and *va* as in va-va-voom. *ivor* as in ignore your mum when she tells you to clean your room, *ko* rhymes with go, and *hov* as in hovercraft. The rest is easy.

Susan George

ISBN 978-0-9956107-4-3

First published August 2017

Illustrations by Laura Woolley

Printed by CZ Design & Print, Bishop's Stortford CM23 3DY

Chapter One

The ENORMOUS Alpha tree stood like an expert ballet dancer at the beginning of a row of twenty-six knowledge trees. The troupe of trees reached out with delicate finger-like branches, each holding hands with the next.

The trees encircled S.N.O.T. Nooooooooooooo, not snot as in from the nose snot. S.N.O.T, the Selheeva Norkohov Open Temple. S.N.O.T was made up of a huge round marble building in which the most miraculous learning took place. A dozen or so smaller round marble buildings branched off the largest and each other to form a warren of wonders. No one would ever, ever, EVER guess what marvels were inside. And no one would ever, ever, EVER guess that the future of such a place could rest on the shoulders of one particularly average little girl called Flora Figaro Turendot Philomena Brain (so called because her mum was a fan of opera), especially not Flora herself, who was at that moment gazing out of the window daydreaming about flying away with the spectacular Sasonga birds. They looked rather like multicoloured lollipops with their huge round heads, huge staring eyes and huge tail feathers. Flora liked lollipops very much.

Shrieks of, "Late for class again, maggot!?" brought Flora momentarily out of her daydream. Headmaster Prickles was on the prowl with his cane and megaphone.

Even the rainbow-plumed lollipop-like Sasonga birds nestling in the branches of the trees surrounding S.N.O.T turned in unison towards the racket. Sounds of scuffling feet and sniffles were heard as the unfortunate child hurried to class. Then it was quiet again; Flora returned to her daydream and the Sasonga birds went back to their nestling.

It turned out that Flora was not the only one who liked lollipops. So did the Temple founder, Dr Selheeva Norkohov. The Sasonga birds appeared at the centre of the school badge, and the colours of the uniform, including scarf, headband, hat and tie, represented the colours of the feathers.

Deep beneath the tranquillity of the treetops a quite spectacular process was taking place at the heart of S.N.O.T. The roots of the twenty-six knowledge trees pirouetted down through the soil, sand and clay, down, down, down until they popped out into the cellar. The cellar of the impressive Selheeva Nokorhov Open Temple rang with the sound of dripping. From the roots and into the barrels below dripped the liquid sap of knowledge. The liquid dripped into the barrels at a speed of a million drips per second.

Drip ... drip ... drip ... drip ... drip ... drip ... drip ... drip ... drip ... drip ... DRIP!

The strong flowery smell seeped into the whitewashed walls of the cellar. Each barrel contained a subject sap, which was stored in subject jugs. Rows and rows of coloured subject jugs holding the precious sap stood on the crooked shelves that lined the curved cellar walls. Professor Spencer Spellman (or Smelly Spelly, as the children and some of the teachers called him due to the pungent stench of rotting flowery BO that clung to him!) was head of chemistry at S.N.O.T. More importantly, he was in charge of making sure that the barrels did not overflow, and that the different subject saps were stored in the correct place and did not get mixed up. It was Cobble and Spit, however, who did all of the hard work. They lived in fear of Spellman, who made them work day and night. The

knowledge sap treatment instructions, written in 1722 by school founder Dr Selheeva Nokorhov himself, were clear: root to barrel, barrel to jug, and jug to brain (after exactly 36.2 days of fermentation). If they deviated just a tiny itsy bit from the instructions, Spellman would punish them.

These two little creatures were raven-like in appearance. Half the size of an average man, they scurried around on skinny, scaly, knobbly kneed legs that were pale as chalk. Their hair was black as a moonless night and slicked back with grease into an Elvis-style quiff. Their beady yellow eyes peered over a large hooked nose and darted left to right, right to left, always on the lookout for anything out of place, anything they could report back to Spellman for a reward of extra feathers to plump up their mattress.

Any child undergoing daily turns on the Steeping Nano Open Temple Seat (or S.N.O.T.S) would learn sensational subject secrets at the speed of sound. Once their brains were exposed, the sap was zapped in at the temple. Their brains, then steeping in the sap, soaked up the subject secrets and a genius emerged! Just as Cobble and Spit slaved under the orders of Spellman, Spellman slaved under the orders of Headmaster Craythorne Prickles. An ex-army colonel, there had never been a stricter, meaner, more child-hating headmaster at S.N.O.T than Craythorne Prickles!

Chapter Two

Prickles had been headmaster at S.N.O.T. for over twenty years. He had decided he disliked all children following an incident with a football and his prize black orchid back in 1967. His position at the Open Temple meant that he could shout at the children and be particularly horrible to them whenever he wanted. It was just like being back in the army and yelling at the new recruits (one of his favourite things). He loved to march through the halls of S.N.O.T, cane under one arm, megaphone at the ready, and parade his authority.

HEADMASTER PRICKLES

"Late for class again, maggot?!" was one of his favourite things to yell at the kids dawdling to class. "Quick march, left, right, left, right, or it will be D.E.T.E.N.T.I.O.N for you!"

If a child was spotted scurrying around the corridors without their blazer on, Prickles gave them a detention. If a child was spotted not wearing their hat, Prickles gave them a detention. Giving out detentions was one of the best things about being headmaster in charge of so many nasty children.

He was paid far too much, and lived rent free in the west wing of the smaller domes that ran off the huge central Temple building. He skimped on the food budget, so the kids got soggy, soppy cabbage and skinny, tasteless, gristly sausages for every meal of every day. The sausages were so gristly they needed a trillion chews before swallowing. If chewing were an Olympic sport, the children of S.N.O.T would win every event. As a treat on Sunday they would just get soggy cabbage, and for dessert a jamless roly-poly pudding with sugar-free custard.

With all the money he saved on food he bought expensive orchids from around the world, like the rare and stunningly beautiful *Phalaenopsis appendiculata*, to add to his collection and show off in competitions. Of course he only bought the best-quality food for them! He frequently treated himself to very expensive handmade silk suits, the softest leather shoes, bow ties and – though he would never admit to wearing one – new wigs.

He was very careful never to be mean in front of the parents or school governors, though. He knew that if the parents complained and stopped paying for their children to attend S.N.O.T, the governors might sack him and he would lose EVERYTHING. Because of this Prickles worked extra hard at perfecting his 'Parent Persona'. He spent hours in front of the mirror every night getting his 'parent' smile just right.

"Corners up, part lips, teeth gleam, eyes twinkle," he chanted to himself over and over again.

More importantly, he knew that if all the children did not pass their knowledge exam at the end of each term there would be no more orchids, and with no orchids there would be no more competitions to enter and no more trophies to add to his gleaming trophy cabinet. In short, his luxury lifestyle would be over forever!

There was one particular little devil who was threatening his lifestyle and that was a certain Flora Figaro Turendot Philomena Brain. The P stood for Philomena, but Headmaster Prickles called her Flora Pea Brain (who could be bothered with all those other silly names!), the girl with a brain the size of a pea. The knowledge sap could be poured and poured into her pea-sized brain and none of it would sink in. It seemed that the more that was poured in, the less she actually knew. Every time Headmaster Prickles thought about Pea Brain, his black bushy caterpillar eyebrows twitched with worry, his frowning forehead frittered, his face turned beetroot red, his temperature rocketed, his fingers curled until his hands were white knuckled fists and his wig wiggled a whole 2 to 3 centimetres forward. How could they force the knowledge into Pea Brain's brain? And failing that, how could they get rid of Pea Brain?

It was all Headmaster Prickles could think about and it was slowly driving him nuts! The end of term was only weeks away, and at the end of term was the end-of-term exam! And where there was an exam paper there was an examiner. The delectable Delores Midthunder would arrive in five weeks. He was sure she hated children almost as much as he did. He had fallen in love with her the first time he met her. He loved everything about her: the way she scraped her fiery red hair into the highest of buns, her throaty Scottish accent, and especially the way she screamed instructions at the 'haggis-brained bernes', as she called the children. He would not let Pea Brain make him look a fool in front of Delores!

Flora was a quiet but confident little girl. She had round, pudgy, pinchable cheeks and chubby little baby-like fingers. She loved chocolate and all bad foods. When she smiled, a row of crooked cream teeth could be seen nestling behind her cherub lips. She was blissfully unaware that the whole of the Selheeva Nokorhov Open Temple set-up could be destroyed if she did not pass the end-of-term knowledge exam.

Chapter Three

Pea Brain was one very sharp thorn in Headmaster Prickles' side, but Miss Daisy Dropfrost was another; all blonde hair, bosoms and long eyelashes. She still believed that all children were sweet and pure. Awful woman! The silly young teacher loved all children as if they were her own. Prickles spent at least an hour each day listening to Dropfrost's list of complaints and the ways in which Prickles could improve the lives of the children in his care.

1. Softer pillows.
2. Softer seating.
3. Less work.
4. More vegetables.
5. More visits from parents.

And on and on the list went…

"I must, must, must, must, MUST get rid of Pea Brain," grumbled Headmaster Pickles.

His black bushy caterpillar eyebrows twitched with worry, his frowning forehead frittered, his face turned beetroot red, his temperature rocketed, his fingers curled until his hands were white knuckled fists and his wig wiggled a whole 2 to 3 centimetres forward. He began to write some of his devilish ideas down on his notepad.

1. Put her in a barrel of leftover cabbage water and lock her in the cellar.
2. Force her to drink deadly nightshade tea.
3. Drop one of the massive slate slabs off the rooftop and flatten her.

He really didn't think any of these were such good ideas. A cabbage-smelling, drowned, poisoned or flattened pupil might not go down too well with the parents and governors.

Then it came to him like a ball through a window smashing a precious orchid! Smallpox! Mumps! Scarlet fever! The plague! If the dreadful child were to come down with some infectious disease, then he would be forced to order her parents to take her away from the school.

He ordered Cobble and Spit to collect two pots of Heapes extremely red, extremely expensive and extremely difficult-to-wash-off paint. Prickles repeated his instructions several times so that the plan was clear to them.

As he watched them scuttle down the corridor mumbling their mantra, "Root to barrel, barrel to jug, jug to brain," their knobbly knees knocking together, he crossed his fingers extra tight and started to imagine how perfect life would be without Pea Brain.

At suppertime Cobble slipped the sleeping solution into Flora's fizzy pop. She was sleeping like a sloth as the clock in the courtyard struck midnight. She snored lightly as Spit painted red dots all over her face, hands and feet.

Flora screamed when she looked in the mirror the following day. Headmaster Prickles loved every moment with Pea Brain and the school nurse, who was absolutely baffled by the symptoms.

"Yes, Mrs Brain, you must, must, must, must, MUST come and pick up your daughter. I cannot put the whole school at risk!" Headmaster Prickles tried to sound concerned about Pea Brain's health, but he found it very hard to keep the delight from his voice.

Heapses extremely red, expensive and difficult-to-wash-off paint washed off in three washes and Flora was back at school the following day. Mrs Brain believed that the naughty children had spotted her daughter's body with red paint. She would never have believed that Headmaster Prickles was involved.

Prickles' ears steamed, his black bushy caterpillar eyebrows twitched, his wig wiggled and his face turned a shade of purple as yet unseen by human eyes when he found out that Flora was back. When he had calmed down a little, he thought about other options. Options that might help repair her leaky brain.

"We must, must, must, must, MUST find the leak," he grumbled to himself.

Headmaster Prickles ordered champagne corks, glue, flour and sticky tape. His idea was based on the method for repairing a leaky bicycle tyre. With the help of Cobble and Spit, they held Flora's head under water in a huge metal bucket until they could see where the little bubbles appeared. Little bubbles appeared everywhere!

As Cobble and Spit held a kicking and squirming Flora down, Prickles began to cork, paste and tape her head.

She was immediately sent to S.N.O.T.S and then back to Headmaster Prickles' office, where he quizzed her on the Latin names of his prize orchids. Before she had even managed to think of *Habenaria radiata* or *Phalaenopsis pantherina*, the liquid knowledge was squirting out all over the place, making her looked like a garden sprinkler. Prickles could feel his eyebrows twitching and wig wiggling.

He stood up and cracked his cane on his desk in despair just as Miss Dropfrost barged in. She had got wind of what was going on and was very cross indeed. She pulled the crying Flora into her rather ample bosom and gave her a huge motherly comforting hug. Glaring at the headmaster through her long eyelashes, who glared back meanly, she vowed to take care of Flora's problem herself.

Chapter Four

The next morning, Flora was met in the S.N.O.T.S by Miss Dropfrost, who was carrying a bicycle pump! Today the liquid was a bright crimson, which meant it was science day. After the usual 30 minutes of steeping and soaking and steeping and soaking, Miss Dropfrost attached the bicycle pump to Flora's brain through the hole in her temple and began to pump.

"This might pinch just a tiny bit, my love," said Miss Dropfrost as she pumped.

"Yikes!" yelped Flora.

"By making the brain bigger … we are giving the sap more of a chance of sticking."

Pump! Pump!

"Yikes!"

"So hopefully you won't leak any more."

Pump … pump … pump!

"Yikes … yikes … YIKES!"

Finally, Miss Dropfrost had pumped enough and she removed the pump from Flora's temple. Flora thought that she might have done too much pumping, as it felt very tight and cramped in her skull. Not at all what she was used to.

After her turn in S.N.O.T.S, Flora entered Smelly Spelly's science lab with no less fear and dread than usual. Her knees knocked like bongos … *BONG!* And her legs shook like plucked guitar strings … *TWANG!* Smelly Spelly was bellowing orders to Cobble and Spit, who were scurrying around, navigating the maze of high chemistry benches with their arms full of small glass bottles containing different coloured powders and potions.

"Root to barrel, barrel to jug, jug to brain," they mumbled, eyes darting left to right, right to left.

The pesky butterflies in Flora's stomach fluttered and flapped around, making her wish she had not had that bag of crisps and bottle of chocolate milkshake for breakfast (courtesy of a food parcel from her gran). She looked nervously at the pots of powders and potions as Smelly Spelly barked instructions for the experiment.

1. Safety goggles on, pigtails pinned to side of head.
2. Pick up blue pot.
3. Shake a sprinkling (a very precise measurement) of powder into large beaker.

Flora concentrated extra hard and followed the instructions carefully.

4. Add a splash of clear liquid from small bottle.
5. Stir.

Flora saw the crimson steam rising from the heads of the other children as they worked, the excess sap evaporating as the knowledge sank in. Clouds of crimson floated around the classroom and the giant extractor fan in the ceiling above them, much bigger than the one her mum had in the kitchen at home, purred into life. It started to suck the steam from the classroom before it fogged up everyone's safety goggles. Without it they would have needed miniature windscreen wipers for their goggles!

Flora carefully stirred her mixture with a long glass rod. Her head started to splutter and spurt, and steam slowly rose up from it. Feeling more confident, she added some of the red powder and more of the clear liquid to her beaker. It turned a lovely purple colour. Steam shot from her head and somersaulted through the air. Was Miss Dropfrost's idea working? Was the knowledge finally sticking?

There was a strange gurgling sound and suddenly, Flora was not so confident any more. Her mixture started spluttering, popping and fizzing ferociously. Before she could do anything, the purple mixture was right up to the top of the beaker, spilling over the side like frothy lava and slithering across the workbench! Her head spluttered, fizzed and popped! The mixture in the beaker popped, spluttered and fizzed!

"Oh no!" she cried as the liquid spurted from her head and her brain shrank back to its normal size after the air hissed out.

Suddenly, there was a loud BANG and the classroom filled with thick purple smoke. The extractor fan went into turbo mode and sucked and sucked until all the smoke was gone.

"FLORA PEA BRAIN!" bellowed Headmaster Prickles, his hairy caterpillar eyebrows twitching ferociously and his wig wiggling so much it practically slipped off his head. "You must, must, must, must, MUST go to D.E.T.E.N.T.I.O.N."

He wacked his cane on the bench in front of her, sending purple gloop flying in all directions.

"Don't worry, Flora," said Miss Dropfrost when she found out what had happened. "Come to my house for tea tonight; I am making my famous vegetable lasagne. We can think of some new ideas there."

Flora really didn't like vegetables. She had never liked them much when she lived at home, but the soggy, sloppy stuff they served up in the dining hall was revolting! In fact, she now hated vegetables so much she hadn't had so much as a bite of broccoli or nibble of carrot in months. She never ate the pongy cabbage or soggy sprouts they served in the S.N.O.T canteen. But after having to write 200 lines of *I must, must, must, must, MUST fix my leaky head in detention*, she wanted to get as far away from Headmaster Prickles as possible. So she agreed, hoping there would be something nice for pudding.

Chapter Five

Everyone was puzzled by Flora's problem, but not everyone was as cross about it as Headmaster Prickles! He lay awake at night thinking of more and more ways to get rid of Pea Brain. He got hardly any sleep, and that made him even more grumpy than usual! When he did sleep, all he dreamt about was her and her watering can of a head! She would be great for watering his prize orchids, he thought, but not much else. Why couldn't she be like all the other perfect, although horrible, children at Selheeva Nokorhov Open Temple? Why did she have to be the only child in the history of the school to have a leak, and why did it have to be now, when he was headmaster? Then there was that busybody Miss Dropfrost. Awful woman! She always showed up when he was tending his orchids. Only the other day she had almost caused him to chop a stem off his prize *Prosthechea Cochleata* when she barged into his office! He had seen her and Flora going off somewhere after Pea Brain's latest detention (he LOVED giving out detentions). He decided he would tell Spellman to order Cobble and Spit to keep a close watch on them for him.

Headmaster Prickles might have thought his ideas to stop Pea Brain's head from leaking were crazy, but Miss Dropfrost was having even crazier ideas. If there had been a competition for crazy ideas, she would definitely win. Miss Dropfrost knew that the headmaster didn't like Flora very much by the way his eyebrows twitched every time he heard her name. After she found out he had made those horrid creatures, Cobble and Spit, paint bright-red polka dots all over her, trying to fake illness, she had given him a good talking to! It was a very good job she didn't know that they had also held her head under water like a punctured bicycle tyre to see where the leak was, or Headmaster Prickles would have had a few punctures himself!

Miss Dropfrost was determined to fix Flora before he could get his hands on her again. So far, nothing they tried had worked. Cotton wool just got soggy, while cheese chunks blocked her ears up so much she couldn't hear and just made the liquid shoot out of the other holes even faster. Flora still had her leak and was bound to fail her exams.

This time they were trying heat, an idea they had come up with after their lovely dinner of vegetable lasagne and fresh crispy salad. Flora would not normally have called any vegetable 'lovely'. Nor would she even have considered putting any salad in her mouth. But when Miss Dropfrost removed the hot steaming lasagne from the oven, the smell was so delicious that Flora's mouth had started watering. Even so, she was not sure it would taste as good as it smelled; but she was wrong, it was better! She even asked for seconds. They both thought the hot water bottle idea was one of the best they had had yet.

Miss Dropfrost thought Flora might have a heater problem. If her brain didn't heat up enough, the excess sap could not evaporate, and the important knowledge would not sink in and stick to her brain. It was Flora who came up with the idea of using a hot water bottle. She had a horrible pink fluffy hot water bottle under her bed that had been a Christmas present from her gran. All the presents she got from her gran were pink and fluffy. Pink was Flora's least favourite colour, but no matter how many times she told her gran, there was always something pink and fluffy wrapped up for her birthday and Christmas.

Flora rushed to Miss Dropfrost's office as soon as she had taken her daily dose of knowledge sap in the Steeping Salon. It had been a muddy brown liquid this morning, which meant geography class.

"I've got the hot water bottle," said Flora as she took a pink fluffy item from her rucksack.

They filled the hot water bottle up, put it on top of Flora's head and quickly pulled a woolly hat over it to hold it in place. The hat was one of those with earflaps that tie under the chin, so there was no chance of it slipping off. Then off she went to geography. She got a few strange looks from the other kids in her class, especially as it was a warm day in the middle of April and definitely not woolly-hat-wearing weather. Sundip, one of the exchange students from S.N.O.T.I (the Temple in India), was particularly confused by it all.

"Aren't you hot under there, Flora?" he asked, his usual bright smile replaced with a look of confusion.

She had tried to explain what she was doing, but the more she talked, the more confused he seemed to get. In the end, she had to give up.

Flora's head got hot all right. At first it seemed to be working. The geography teacher was thrilled when she got the first two questions right, but then it all went wrong.

"What is the capital city of France?" he asked her.

"Barcelona," she said proudly, sure she was right.

"Barcelona? Barcelona? No, no, no, my girl, it is Paris! What is the capital city of Germany?" he asked, hopeful she would get the right answer.

"Warsaw," said Flora, starting to feel a little unsure of herself.

"Warsaw? Warsaw? No, no, no, my girl, it is Berlin!"

And on it went, with Flora getting question after question wrong. The only thing the hot water bottle did was give her a sweaty head and frizzy hair! And worst of all, she bumped into Headmaster Prickles in the corridor after class and he gave her another detention for inappropriate headwear.

"You must, must, must, must, MUST go to my office at the D.O.U.B.L.E!" he shouted, eyebrows twitching and wig wiggling. "Quick march, quick march," he yelled all the way.

She had to write 200 lines of *I must, must, must, must, MUST not wear fluffy pink hot water bottles on my head*, before he let her go.

Back in Miss Dropfrost's office, Flora couldn't stop the tears.

"What are we going to do?" she blubbed. "My head is still leaky, and now it's all sweaty and frizzy too. And my hand aches from writing all those lines."

Miss Dropfrost was calm, as usual.

"Here, have a nice piece of courgette and beetroot chocolate cake while we look through our list and decide what to try next."

Flora was not at all keen on the sound of cake with courgette in it! And beetroot ... YUK! I mean, who has heard of such a thing? But when she saw the lashings of chocolate icing on top she couldn't resist having a big bite. And it was delicious.

Chapter Six

That night, Flora lay in bed feeling much better, her stomach full of delicious courgette and beetroot chocolate cake! Who knew courgette and beetroot could be so yummy? The cake was so soft and moist and (best of all) chocolatey that Flora had asked for seconds. Of course Miss Dropfrost had insisted she have some 'proper food' first and they had gone back to her house for a chicken salad.

"You did get *some* questions right, though," Miss Dropfrost had reassured her over their second slice of cake. "That is progress, so something must be working."

They had looked through their list of ideas and chosen such a crazy one that it might just work. Flora would have to make sure she stayed out of Headmaster Prickles' way tomorrow. If he thought a fluffy pink hot water bottle was inappropriate headwear, he was not going to like the octopus much!

That's right, an octopus. A baby octopus to be exact, two of them. It was Headmaster Prickles and his blasted orchids that had given Miss Dropfrost the idea. He had given her a long lecture about his *Prosthechea Cochleata* orchid, which looked just like an octopus with its long tentacle-like petals.

Miss Dropfrost happened to have a friend who worked at an aquarium and had borrowed the baby octopuses for the biology teacher to show her class.

"We can stick their suction pads over all the leaks. With eight tentacles each and who knows how many suction pads per tentacle, there should be plenty to cover them all and still be some left over," Miss Dropfrost explained.

All night Flora dreamed she was an octopus living in the cool blue sea and woke up feeling calm and refreshed.

That feeling did not last long, though. With her head filled of lime-green knowledge sap (the colour of maths), she went to find Miss Dropfrost in the biology lab.

"They have a very tight grip," said the biology teacher as they were sticking the tentacles to Flora's head, one over each ear. "I got one stuck to my arm in class the other day. Took twenty-three of us to peel him off!" She laughed.

Flora was becoming less sure about the whole thing by the minute. She could feel the suction pads gripping her head. *This must be what a car feels like before it gets crushed in one of those giant machines*, she thought.

Off Flora went, with an octopus over each ear, tentacles splayed over her head like some living spaghetti hat and water spray in hand (to keep the octopuses moist). The looks she got from the kids in her geography class were nothing compared to those from the kids in her maths class. This time she didn't even try to explain what was going on to Sundip.

"Yes, Flora, 19 x 3 is 57!" the maths teacher said happily.

Again and again Flora put her hand up to answer his questions, and again and again she got them right. It was not until the end of class that she felt a trickle down her neck. At first she thought it was one of the octopuses tickling her, but then she started to get the questions wrong.

"Wrong, 6 + 11 is not 20! … Wrong, 20 – 13 is not 4!"

Flora did not see Headmaster Prickles on her way back to the biology lab, but she did see those awful creatures, Cobble and Spit. It was a rare occasion them not being under the watchful eye of Smelly Spelly, but she knew they would be racing back to tell him what they had seen and it would not be long before they were in Headmaster Prickles' office blathering away. If Headmaster Prickles saw her, his eyebrows would surely shoot right off his face and never come back, and she would be in detention for the rest of her natural life!

Back in the biology lab, they rushed to prise the octopuses off her head. Flora held on tight to the back of a chair as Miss Dropfrost and the biology teacher pulled and pulled and pulled. With one foot each on a desk for more leverage, they heaved and heaved and heaved. Finally, with a *SHLERP!*, Flora was free. The two teachers staggered backwards and landed with a bump on their bottoms. Hands over heads, they struggled to keep hold of the octopuses and their wiggling, waving tentacles. They managed to get them back in their tank just in the nick of time as Headmaster Prickles burst through the door like a mad bull caught in a tornado. Catching a glimpse of Flora's octopusless head, he snorted and muttered something about orchids before leaving quickly. It was a good job he did not look too closely, otherwise he would have seen the little round red marks all over Flora's face left by the suction pads.

"Progress, Flora!" exclaimed Miss Dropfrost as she pulled her in for a hug and squished her up against her ample bosom. "We are making progress. We just have to work out what it is that we are doing right."

The octopuses were returned to their tank at the aquarium where, over the next few days, they started exhibiting very strange behaviour indeed. One octopus would carefully pick out the green stones from the gravel in the tank and make two piles, whilst the other would pick out the blue stones and make another pile. They kept doing this, discarding some stones and then adding more. It was soon discovered that one was setting math problems and the other was solving them. They had absorbed some of the math knowledge sap and were now genius octopus mathematicians. Within a week they were the top attraction at the aquarium, with people coming from far and wide to see them. Since then, Miss Dropfrost had said it was best they steer clear of using live animals.

"Well, Flora, it seems that we do our best thinking when eating. How does pizza sound, with extra mushrooms and red peppers?"

Flora loved pizza, but mushrooms and peppers were definitely not her usual topping. Three cheese with extra cheese and pepperoni was her favourite. But just like everything that Miss Dropfrost made, it was delicious.

Try as they might, they could not think of how hot water bottles and octopuses together had made Flora's leaking problem start to go away.

"It's probably all this delicious food you are feeding me, Miss Dropfost," joked Flora. "It is so much nicer than the food they serve in the dining hall at S.N.O.T. I never normally eat any of the soggy, pongy vegetables."

At that moment a light bulb came on in Miss Dropfrost's brain and a curious look came over her face.

"Another slice, dear?" she asked.

Perhaps those old wives tales are true, thought Miss Dropfrost after Flora had gone back to the dorm. You are what you eat, 5-a-day to keep the doctor away, and all that. Perhaps carrots really could help you see in the dark!

Chapter Seven

It was the week of the end-of-term exams! The trees had been watered and fed, pruned and pricked. Liquid knowledge production had doubled in the past three weeks and Headmaster Prickles had ordered the children to spend double the time on the S.N.O.T.S, soaking up the knowledge. Pea Brain was given an extra four hours.

"Report, Dropfrost! What have you got to say for yourself and that leaky Pea Brain?"

Miss Dropfrost put her idea about the vegetables to the headmaster.

"This is all your fault, you know. If you spent money on some decent food for these children and served them nice crunchy vegetables and crisp salad instead of those soggy, pongy cabbage and sprouts, this might not have happened."

Headmaster Prickles thought she was talking nonsense, but other than locking Flora in a cupboard he was out of options. So he ordered her to force-feed Flora vegetables and salad for every meal. Of course, she didn't need to force-feed her at all, as Flora gladly ate all the delicious food Miss Dropfrost gave her.

The governors arrived just before noon on the day of the exam. They prowled the examination room like cats ganging up on tiny mice. The children sat in rows and Miss Dropfrost hovered at the front of the room, sending out smiles and comforting thumbs-up.

All temples were secured and the children were told to fill in the answers on the very, very long question paper.

"If anyone is caught cheating, EVERYONE will fail!" boomed the strictly efficient Delores Midthunder. "You may begin," she said, her nose in the air.

Oh, how she loved to see the children taking exams, their little heads down and pencils scribbling like crazy. Seeing young minds at work was one of her favourite things.

There was a flapping of overturned pages, and the children bowed their heads and scanned the paper. Pens and pencils began to scratch answers.

The silence in the room was spooky. Every now and again a chair squeaked, a pencil snapped or a child coughed. All movements were closely monitored by Delores. When anyone sneezed, Miss Dropfrost ran to his or her side with tissues.

Towards the end of the exam, Headmaster Prickles appeared at the doorway. He became alarmed when he saw that Pea Brain was sitting motionless at her table.

I just knew those vegetables weren't going to work, he thought to himself. Close to tears, he sneaked back to his office, his twitching eyebrows and wiggling wig now frozen in fear.

Chapter Eight

"You must put your pens down now, RIGHT NOW!" thundered Delores Midthunder in a voice even scarier and almost as loud as real thunder.

It is as if Flora never actually picked up her pen in the first place, thought Miss Dropfrost in silent desperation. Nevertheless, she managed to appear upbeat.

"Well done, my little angels," she said, smiling sweetly. "A special lunch awaits you in the S.N.O.T dining hall."

There was a clatter, clash and clank as children moved chairs. The children were so tired and hungry. Delores Midthunder gathered up the exam papers, strutting up and down between the rows of desks. Miss Dropfrost tried to speak over the tired chatter. She reminded the children that the results would be pinned on the noticeboard at 5 p.m. It was going to be a very tense few hours.

Miss Dropfrost couldn't bear to just sit and wait for the results to be posted, and she decided to use the hours wisely. She had constantly complained to the headmaster about the lack of decent fresh vegetables in the dining hall. He had never taken her complaints seriously, though, so she thought she would do a little investigation of her own. The head cook welcomed her into her kitchen. All of the staff loved Miss Dropfrost. The cook willingly explained the difficulties of working with such a tiny budget.

"2p per child for each meal," she said.

That certainly explained the soggy cabbage and pongy sprouts.

Miss Dropfrost decided to seek out Delores Midthunder. She might look and sound very scary, but Miss Dropfrost knew that she only wanted the best for the children. They were both very good with numbers and only needed to spend 30 minutes with the accounts to see what was happening. The poor cook had often given money out of her own pocket to swell the supplies. Miss Dropfrost and Delores were horrified with what was going on and were determined to do something about it.

No one could get an appointment with Headmaster Prickles that afternoon. A huge 'Do not disturb' sign hung across his door. Prickles sat transfixed, the clock in his line of sight. He mentally made a note of all the changes he would be forced to make should Pea Brain fail. Not even his prize orchids could make him feel any better.

The clock struck two … three … four … and then the dreaded hour arrived. Everyone in the school made their way to the noticeboard. Even Cobble and Spit. Everyone, that is, except the headmaster.

Flora looked at the list. She looked and blinked and blinked and looked. She looked and blinked and squealed. It was a squeal of delight.

"Oh, my little cabbage!" shrieked Miss Dropfrost in disbelief.

She hugged Flora so tight the poor child turned a pale shade of magenta.

Delores Midthunder cried with proud satisfaction.

Flora sniffed with delight.

And so it was that with a shriek, a cry and a sniff, S.N.O.T was saved.

The large gaggle of students and staff turned as one when a taxi pulled into the S.N.O.T car park. They were all rather astonished to see the headmaster struggling over to the taxi with a suitcase and an armful of large orchids.

He was under a constant barrage from the Sasonga birds, who were determined to make off with his orchids. Miss Dropfrost recognised the *Prosthechea Cochleata* as it vanished into the trees and stifled a laugh. Even Smelly Spelly, Cobble and Spit could not hide their delight.

Delores clapped her hands to draw everyone's attention from the swiftly departing taxi.

"May I introduce your new headmistress," she exclaimed, pointing to the lovely Miss Dropfrost.